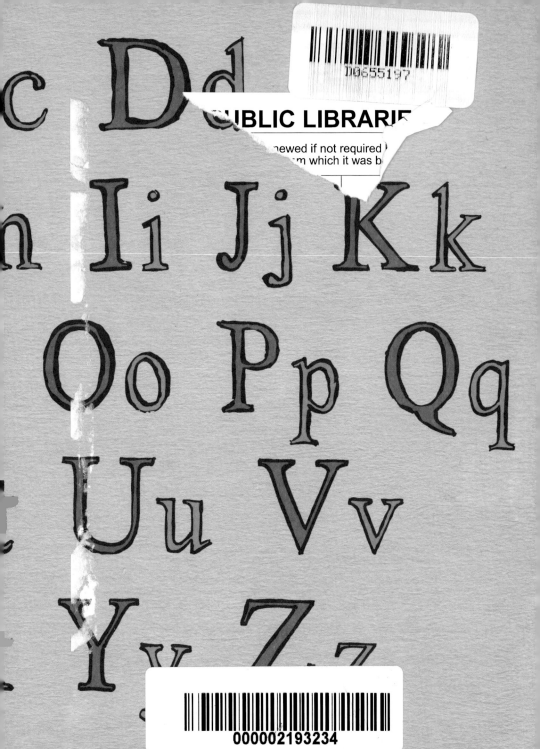

This alphabet was inspired by original paintings of Luke's children and by the woodcuts of William Nicholson. As in traditional alphabets, every letter is illustrated by a simple object or action. Running alongside, Kate's poem takes a less literal approach, responding to the mood of each picture in a loosely rhymed celebration of childhood.

Every Girl's Alphabet

Kate Bingham Luke Martineau

GRAFFEG

Every girl is up for adventure.

Every girl best be prepared.

Every girl is a curious creature.

Keeping her distance,
every girl dares.

Every girl likes making
an entrance,

acting up to please her fans.

Every girl has a gift
she'll grow into.

Every girl holds your heart
in her hands.

Every girl takes care
of what's important.

Life is a journey
of ups and downs.

Every girl will keep on trying,

or learn to live
with her feet on the ground.

Every girl acts
on the spur of the moment.

Every nightingale knows
when she's needed.

Every girl needs a world
of her own,

every plan to be completed.

Every girl is quick to question.

Every girl runs
till her legs are hollow.

Every girl feels the stretch
in her wings.

Every girl looks out
for tomorrow.

Unafraid of ugly weather,

every girl will voice her views.

Every wonder of the world

exhausts at last her last excuse.

Another yawn, another day

unfolds itself from Z to A.

Every Girl's Alphabet

Every girl is up for adventure.
Every girl best be prepared.
Every girl is a curious creature.
Keeping her distance, every girl dares.
Every girl likes making an entrance,
acting up to please her fans.
Every girl has a gift she'll grow into.
Every girl holds your heart in her hands.
Every girl takes care of what's important.
Life is a journey of ups and downs.
Every girl will keep on trying,
or learn to live with her feet on the ground.
Every girl acts on the spur of the moment.
Every nightingale knows when she's needed.
Every girl needs a world of her own,
every plan to be completed.
Every girl is quick to question.
Every girl runs till her legs are hollow.
Every girl feels the stretch in her wings.
Every girl looks out for tomorrow.
Unafraid of ugly weather,
every girl will voice her views.
Every wonder of the world
exhausts at last her last excuse.
Another yawn, another day
unfolds itself from Z to A.

Unique, inquisitive and endlessly imaginative, every boy is an action hero in this modern alphabet of childhood. The affection visible in Luke Martineau's fluid illustrations is matched by Kate Bingham's tender, witty poem, written to appeal to adults as much as to the puzzling younger mind.

Available from all good bookshops and
online at www.graffeg.com

About the authors

Kate Bingham has published two novels and three books of poetry: *Cohabitation, Quicksand Beach* and *Infragreen*. She was shortlisted for the Forward Prize in 2006 and 2010, and her newest poems can sometimes be found in the TLS and the Spectator. Read more about her work at katebingham.com.

Luke Martineau is a painter of informal family portraits, landscapes and still life. For 25 years he has exhibited in London, where he lives. When not drawing inspiration from his own family, painting trips have taken him to Sweden, Germany, Italy, the US, Cambodia, Hong Kong and India. He is currently President of Chelsea Art Society. See more about Luke at lukemartineau.com.

Luke and Kate have been friends since they were students, and this collaboration has grown in step with their own children, some of whom are now students themselves.

Kate Holland is a multi-award winning bookbinder, specialising in contemporary fine binding to commission. Her books are held in the collections of the British, Bodleian and Yale University Libraries, amongst others. Much of the design, layout and typesetting of this book is her work. Limited editions, signed by the authors, are available at katehollandbooks.co.uk.

Every Girl's Alphabet
Published in Great Britain in 2018
by Graffeg Limited.

Written by Kate Bingham
copyright © 2010. Illustrated by Luke
Martineau copyright © 2010. Designed by
Kate Holland © 2017. Designed and produced
by Graffeg Limited copyright © 2018.

Graffeg Limited, 24 Stradey Park Business
Centre, Mwrwg Road, Llangennech, Llanelli,
Carmarthenshire SA14 8YP Wales UK
Tel 01554 824000 www.graffeg.com

ISBN 9781912654536

1 2 3 4 5 6 7 8 9

Aa Bb C

Ff Gg H

Ll Mm Nr

Rr Ss T

Ww X